# Table of Contents

I See Family ........................... 3

Photo Glossary ..................... 14

About the Authors/
Photographers ..................... 15

# Can You Find These Words?

cooking

family

gardening

pets

# I See Family

family

I see **family** in day trips.

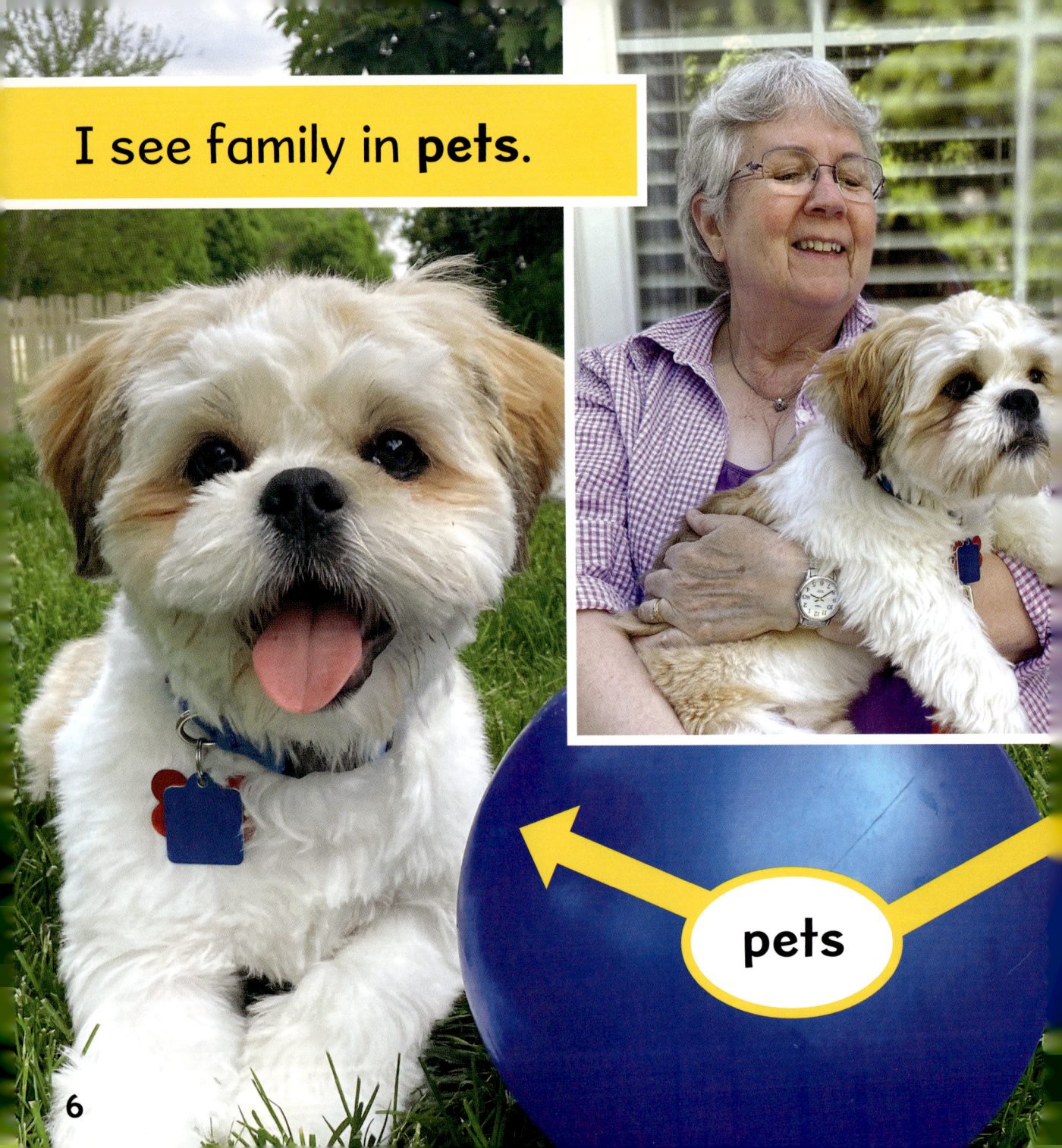

I see family in **pets**.

pets

I see family in **gardening** together.

I see family in traditions.

# Photo Glossary

 **cooking** (kuk-ing): Preparing and heating food for eating.

 **family** (FAM-uh-lee): A group of people related to one another.

 **gardening** (GAHR-duhn-ing): Growing or taking care of plants in a garden.

 **pets** (petz): Tame animals kept for company and treated with affection.

# About the Authors/Photographers

Alma Patricia Ramirez is a writer who enjoys writing in English and Spanish for children and adults. She enjoys time with her family. Some of her favorite family activities are hiking, baking, cooking, and celebrating traditions.

Allen R. Wells is a writer and mechanical engineer in Atlanta, GA. He is excited to share the things he enjoys doing with family.

Kaitlyn Duling is a writer and editor. She loves spending time with her brother, sister, and parents. Kaitlyn lives with her wife in Washington, DC.

Martin Wong is a writer who lives in Los Angeles, California. He weaves family into everything he does, from work and play to art and organizing.

© 2022 Published by Rourke Educational Media. No part of this book may be reproduced or utilized in any form or by any means, electronic or mechanical including photocopying, recording, or by any information storage and retrieval system without permission in writing from the publisher.

www.rourkebooks.com

PHOTO CREDITS: cover: (background) ©Getty Images; cover, page 2, 4, 5, 12, 13, 14, 15: Alma Patricia Ramirez; page 2, 8, 9, 14, 15: Allen R. Wells; page 2, 6, 7, 14, 15: Kaitlyn Duling; page 2, 3, 10, 11, 14, 15: Martin Wong

Edited by: Hailey Scragg
Cover and interior design by: Lynne Schwaner

**Library of Congress PCN Data**
I See Family/ Alma Patricia Ramirez, Kaitlyn Duling, Allen R. Wells, Martin Wong
(Life Through My Lens)
ISBN 978-1-73165-187-7 (hard cover)
ISBN 978-1-73165-232-4 (soft cover)
ISBN 978-1-73165-202-7 (E-book)
ISBN 978-1-73165-217-1 (e-Pub)

Library of Congress Control Number: 2021944578

Printed in Ningbo, Zhejiang, China
04-0202512936